# Ellie: The Perfect Dress for Me

By C.M. Rubin

Illustrated by Christopher Fowler

Columbus, Ohio

To every little girl who has a passion for clothes.
To my family for supporting mine.
C. M. Rubin

To the faculty and students of Lura B. Kean Elementary School
C. F.

Text © 2006 C.M. Rubin
Art © 2006 Dancing Penguins, LLC

This edition published in the United States of America in 2006 by Gingham Dog Press, an imprint of School Specialty Publishing, a member of the School Specialty Family.

**A Dancing Penguins, LLC/J. R. Sansevere Book**

www.SchoolSpecialtyPublishing.com

Library of Congress Cataloging-in-Publication Data is on file with the publisher.

Printed in The United States of America.
Send all inquiries to:
School Specialty Publishing
8720 Orion Place
Columbus, Ohio 43240-2111

ISBN 0-7696-3299-8

1 2 3 4 5 6 7 8 9 10 PHXBK 10 09 08 07 06 05

It all began on April 4.
An invitation reached our door.
It looked so great,
I could not wait
to hear what lay in store.

There was to be a grand affair—
the wedding of our cousin Claire.
The bridegroom was a billionaire,
who came from Greenville, Delaware.

Mom called him "suave"
and "debonair,"
the son of Lord Horatio Blair,
himself a multi-millionaire.

And so she said, "No time to spare.
We've much to do,
things to prepare.
Of course, they've also asked the Mayor
and Governor.
I do declare,
the President is flying there!
There will be cameras everywhere!

So what
is Ellie going to wear?"

My new friend, Arabella Jewel,
likes to follow just one rule.
When a girl has got to dress,
think  MORE!

It's much more fun than less.
More baubles, bangles, beads, and pearls,
tiaras, trinkets, clips and curls.
A dress with less is just a waste.
A dress with much more fun has taste!

The dress revealed
a true princess.
The dress with
much more fun than less.

But, *boi-yong, boi-yong,* beads hit the floor!
*Boi-yong, boi-yong,* came thirty more!
Then, as she tried to make them stop,
her gold tiara went *ka-plop,*
and knocked those
trinkets, clips and curls,
and lots more baubles,
beads, and pearls!

Alas, it seemed a tragic waste
for such a dress with so much taste!

Papa says,
"Now, let me see.
Why don't we dress
you up like me?
In hat and tails
and silver tie,
you'll look so smooth
that folks will cry,

'Wow, see that girl who's standing there?
She's like that dancer Fred Astaire!'
In hat and tails,
you just won't stop.
You'll dance and dance
until you drop!"

The girl who looked like Fred Astaire
in hat and tails was standing there.
She clicked her fingers—*snap snap snap*.
Her feet must follow—*tap tap tap*.

Across the tables
to the floor,
the walls, the ceiling,
chairs, and more!

In hat and tails,
she never stops.
You have to wait
until she drops!

Nana's picked me an old gown
in cream and white
and golden brown

that great, great, great,
great Nana Kate
wore when she
was almost eight.
And so she says,
now that it's mine,

"Remember that it's frail and fine.
No sudden thrills
or little spills.
You'll spoil the lace
and rip those frills."

"I'm sure," says Nana,
"that you will
be very poised
and very still!"

The DJ said, "There's *just* no chance.
The little girl will want to dance.
A sudden thrill
could rip her frill.
She *must* be poised.
She *must* stand still."

And do not think
she'll sip her drink,
because that will
produce a spill.
She *must* be poised.
She *must* stand still.

A doctor might be called to see
what kind of sickness this could be.
Perhaps a chill, she looks so ill—
so very still!

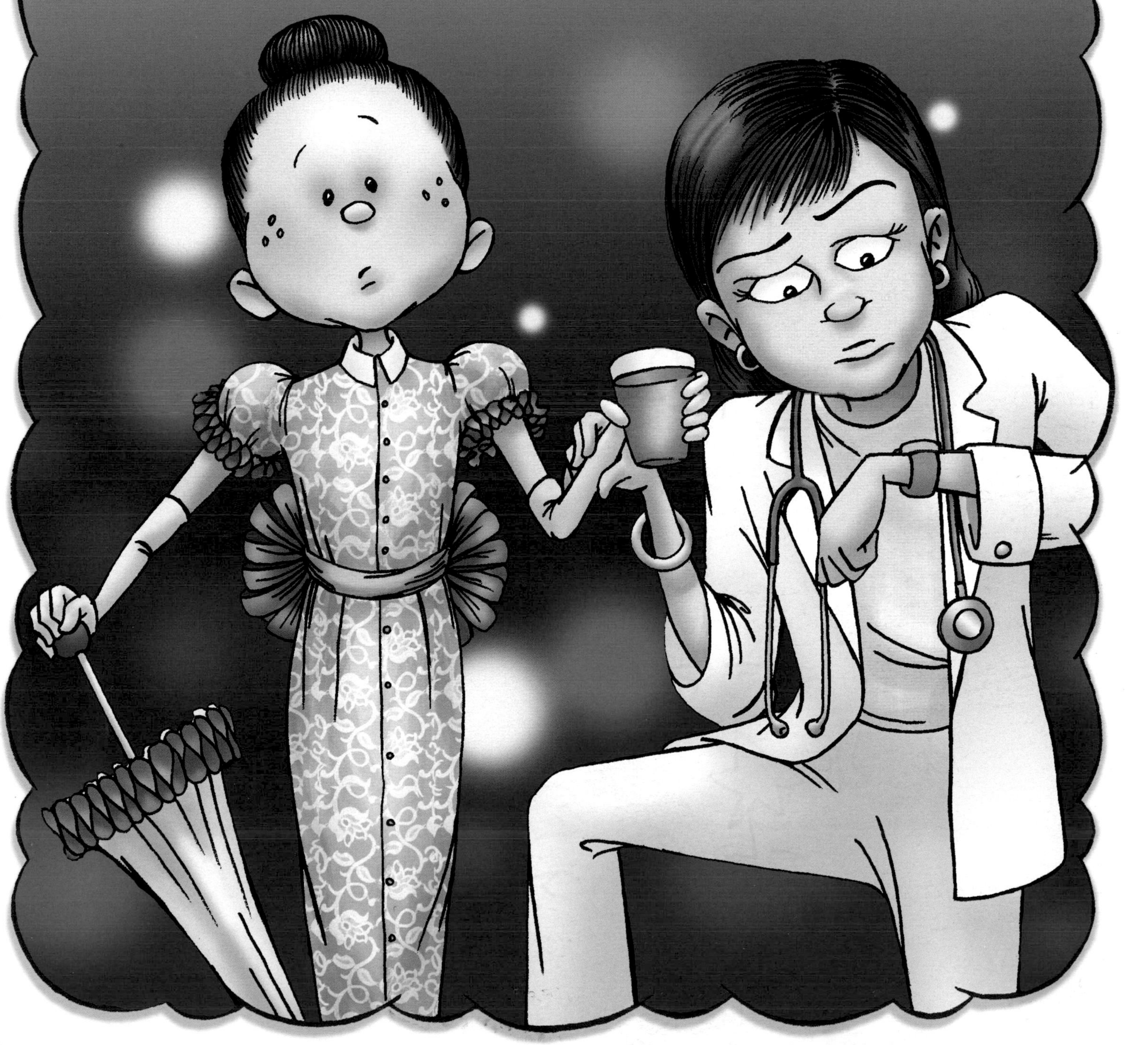

Mom took me on a trip today to meet Coco McCall,
who told me there were many times when she was very small,
she didn't like the dresses
folks would make her wear at all.

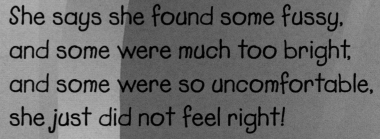

She says she found some fussy,
and some were much too bright,
and some were so uncomfortable,
she just did not feel right!

And so Coco decided,
in nineteen ninety-three,
to open up a store
that's called
"The Perfect Dress for Me."

Well, now dear Mom's designing—
morning, noon, and night—
an absolutely brilliant dress
in which I shall look right.

She's picked out lovely fabrics.
She's browsed through many books.
My mom has many big ideas
for many different looks.
But yet, poor Mom is struggling—
it's such a grand affair.
Before we pick the perfect dress,
what color shall I wear?

Yummy in yellow
or gorgeous in green?
Outrageous in orange
with hot pink between?

Then
early this morning,
Mom bounced on my bed.
"I've got it!" she bellowed,

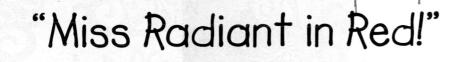

"Miss Radiant in Red!"

And suddenly
they saw a light—
a blinding sight—
that glared so bright.
"What's that ahead?"
the bridegroom said.
It was—

Miss
Radiant
in Red!

Her dress glowed like a burning beam.
It was so shockingly extreme!
And people fled.
They seemed to dread
that girl—

# Miss Radiant in Red!

The bridesmaids
screamed,
"Take her away!"
The bride cried,
"She has wrecked my day!"

and—still unwed—was sent to bed,
thanks to Miss Radiant in Red!

Enough!

I was determined.
They must leave me alone

to think about this perfect dress
entirely on my own.

And for the very grand affair, I made the dress I chose to wear.
"Great job," said the President. "I like your dress. It's excellent."

My family were by my side.
They said their hearts were full of pride.

And my delight was
hard to hide,
since everyone could see,
this really was
the perfect dress . . .